Christmas   1989

Chris, Lindsay, Lauren

Merry Christmas from

Aunt Marsha & Uncle Steve

Blossom
Comes Home

James Herriot

Illustrated by Ruth Brown

St Martin's Press
New York

© 1972, 1988 by James Herriot   Illustrations © 1988 Ruth Brown   ISBN 0–312–02169–0 LCN 88–12017

I arrived at Mr Dakin's farm just outside Darrowby on a warm
April morning. The green hillside ran down to the river, and
the spring sunshine danced on the water. The birds were singing
and lambs played on the flower-strewn pastures.

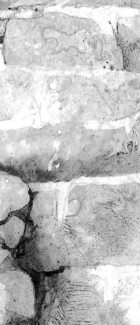

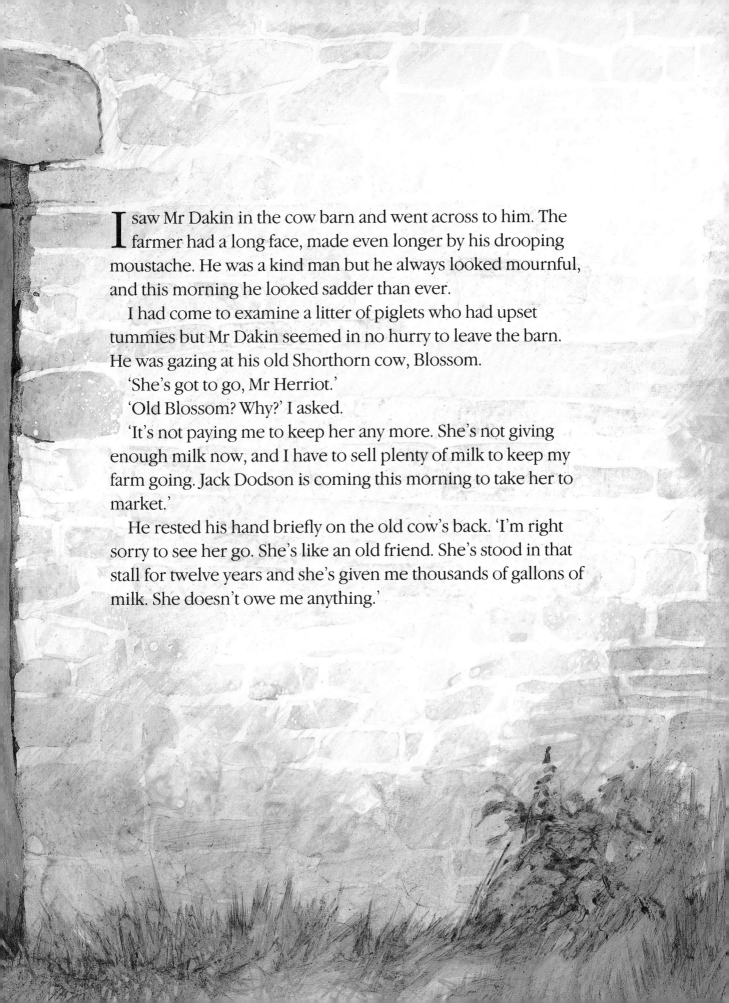

I saw Mr Dakin in the cow barn and went across to him. The farmer had a long face, made even longer by his drooping moustache. He was a kind man but he always looked mournful, and this morning he looked sadder than ever.

I had come to examine a litter of piglets who had upset tummies but Mr Dakin seemed in no hurry to leave the barn. He was gazing at his old Shorthorn cow, Blossom.

'She's got to go, Mr Herriot.'

'Old Blossom? Why?' I asked.

'It's not paying me to keep her any more. She's not giving enough milk now, and I have to sell plenty of milk to keep my farm going. Jack Dodson is coming this morning to take her to market.'

He rested his hand briefly on the old cow's back. 'I'm right sorry to see her go. She's like an old friend. She's stood in that stall for twelve years and she's given me thousands of gallons of milk. She doesn't owe me anything.'

There were only six cows in the old cobbled barn with its low roof and wooden partitions, and they all had names. You don't find cows with names any more, and there aren't many farmers like Mr Dakin who somehow scratch a living from a herd of six milking cows and a few calves, pigs and hens.

As if she knew she were the topic of conversation, Blossom turned her head and looked at him. She was certainly very ancient: her pelvic bones jutted out from her skinny body and her udder drooped almost to the ground. But there was something appealing in the friendliness of the eyes and the patient expression on her face.

Mr Dakin had fallen silent as he looked fondly at his cow. I was about to suggest that we might see the piglets when I heard a clattering of boots in the yard and Jack Dodson, the cattle-drover, hurried into the barn.

'Now then, Mr Dakin,' he cried. 'It's easy to see which one you want me to take. It's that skinny old thing over there.'

He pointed to Blossom and, in truth, the unkind description seemed to fit the bony creature standing among her sleek neighbours.

The farmer didn't reply for a moment, then he went between the cows and gently rubbed Blossom's forehead. 'Aye, this is the one, Jack.' Then he undid the chain round her neck. 'Off you go, old lass,' he murmured, and the cow turned and made her way placidly from the stall.

'Come along, come along!' shouted Jack Dodson, prodding the cow's rump.

'Don't hit her!' barked Mr Dakin.

Mr Dodson looked at him in surprise. 'I never hit 'em, you know that. Just help 'em along, like.'

'All right,' Mr Dakin replied. 'But you won't need your stick for this one. She'll go wherever you want, always has done.'

Blossom proved him right and ambled across the yard. She turned up the track to join a group of fat bullocks and cows standing on the road high above. A boy and a dog circled them, keeping them together.

The farmer and I stood watching as Blossom made her way unhurriedly up the hill, Jack Dodson following behind her. As the path wound behind an old grey barn, man and beast disappeared – but Mr Dakin still gazed after them, listening to the clip-clop of the hooves on the hard ground.

When the sound had died away, he turned to me quickly. 'Right, Mr Herriot, we'll get on with seeing those little pigs.'

There were twelve squealing piglets in the sty with their mother. The farmer gently picked each one up and held it while I gave it an injection which would make it better. This took me about fifteen minutes and I tried to pass the time by talking about the weather, cricket matches and other things, but Mr Dakin replied only with a series of grunts. I could see that he was still sad about Blossom.

I, too, was thinking about the old cow as I drove away from the farm, up the track and on to the road above. On my way home, I had to pass through the nearby village of Briston, and as I arrived, I saw the herd of cattle at the far end of the street. Mr Dodson was making another collection, and the boy was chatting to some friends by the roadside. I could see Blossom at the rear of the group, with her head turned, looking back.

Briston was where Mrs Pickering lived with her three Basset hounds and Buster, the cat who was once her Christmas Day kitten. One of the dogs had broken his leg a month before and I had to remove the plaster cast this morning.

I lifted the dog on to the table and while I was cutting away the plaster, Buster kept frisking around, pawing playfully at my hand as the solemn-faced Bassets looked on disapprovingly.

After I had taken off the cast, I could see that the leg had set very well. 'He'll be fine now, Mrs Pickering,' I said.

Just then, I saw a single unattended cow trot past the window. This was unusual because cows always have somebody in charge and, anyway, there was something familiar about this one. I hurried to the window and looked out. It was Blossom!

'Please excuse me,' I said to Mrs Pickering. I packed my bag quickly, and rushed out to my car.

B lossom was moving down the village street at a good pace, her eyes fixed steadily ahead as though she were going somewhere important. What on earth had happened? She should have been at Darrowby market by now. People in the street were staring at her and the postman nearly fell off his bike as she pushed past him. Then she disappeared round the corner and out of sight.

I had to turn the car, and then I drove after her at top speed – but when I rounded the corner, there was no sign of her, and the road that stretched ahead of me was empty. She had vanished – but where had she gone?

One thing was certain. I had to go back to Mr Dakin's farm and tell him that Blossom had broken away and was loose in the countryside.

I urged my little car as fast as I could and when I reached the farm, I met Mr Dakin carrying a sack of grain across the yard.

He looked at me in surprise 'Hello, Mr Herriot. Have you forgotten something?'

I was about to blurt out my story when he raised his head suddenly, and listened. 'What's that?' he said.

From somewhere on the hillside above us, I could hear the clip-clop of hooves. As we stood in the yard and listened, a cow rounded a rocky outcrop and came towards us. It was Blossom, moving at a brisk trot, great udder swinging, eyes fixed purposefully on the barn door.

'What on earth. . .' burst out Mr Dakin, but the old cow brushed past us and marched without hesitation into the stall she had occupied for the past twelve years. She sniffed enquiringly at the empty hay rack and looked round at her astonished owner.

Mr Dakin stared back at her. The eyes in the weathered face were watery, and he began to pull thoughtfully at his long moustache.

The silence was broken by the sound of heavy boots on the cobbles of the yard, and Jack Dodson panted his way through the door.

'Oh, there you are, you old scallywag!' he gasped. 'I'm right sorry, Mr Dakin. I left that lad in charge for a few minutes and he let her escape.' Then he moved towards Blossom. 'Come on, lass, let's be having you out of there.'

But he halted as Mr Dakin held an arm in front of him.

There was a long silence as Dodson looked in surprise at the farmer who continued to gaze at the cow. There was a quiet dignity about the old animal as she stood there against the crumbling timbers of the partition, her eyes patient and undemanding.

Then, still without speaking, Mr Dakin moved unhurriedly between the cows and the faint click of metal sounded as he fastened the chain around Blossom's neck. Next he strolled to the end of the barn and returned with a forkful of hay which he tossed expertly into the wooden rack.

This was what Blossom was waiting for. She snatched a mouthful and began to chew with quiet satisfaction.

W hat's going on?' cried Jack Dodson in bewilderment.
 'I'll be late for market.'
'I'm sorry I've wasted your time, Jack,' the farmer replied
owly, 'but you'll have to go without her.'
'Without her... but...?' spluttered Mr Dodson.
'Aye, you'll think I'm daft, but that's how it is. The old lass has
me home and she's staying home.'
 Mr Dodson shook his head, and left to get back to the market.

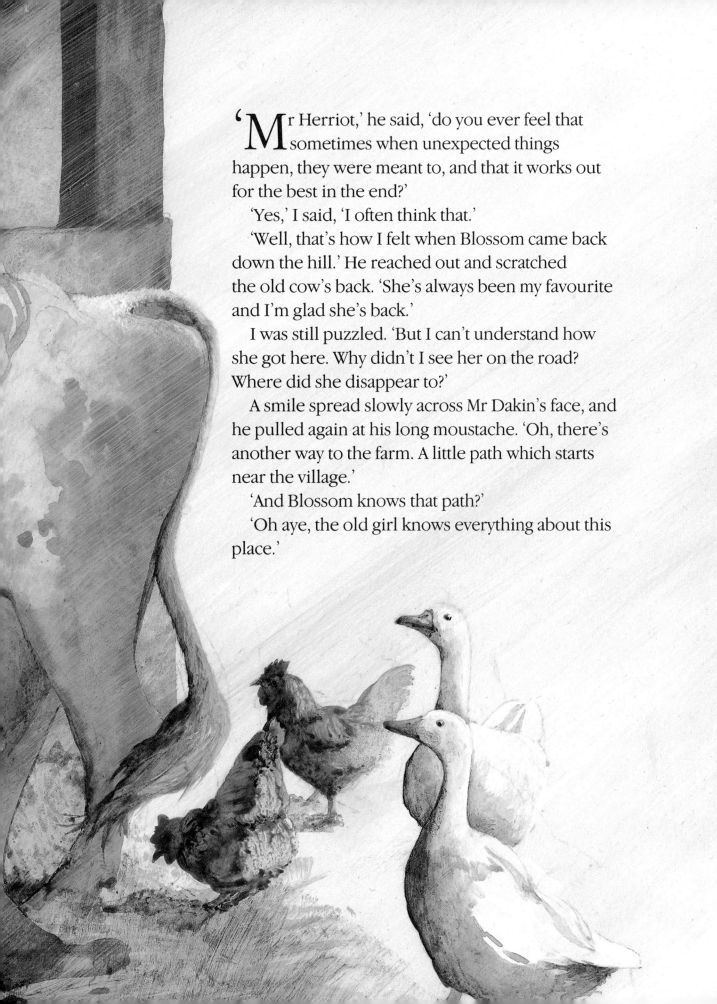

'Mr Herriot,' he said, 'do you ever feel that sometimes when unexpected things happen, they were meant to, and that it works out for the best in the end?'

'Yes,' I said, 'I often think that.'

'Well, that's how I felt when Blossom came back down the hill.' He reached out and scratched the old cow's back. 'She's always been my favourite and I'm glad she's back.'

I was still puzzled. 'But I can't understand how she got here. Why didn't I see her on the road? Where did she disappear to?'

A smile spread slowly across Mr Dakin's face, and he pulled again at his long moustache. 'Oh, there's another way to the farm. A little path which starts near the village.'

'And Blossom knows that path?'

'Oh aye, the old girl knows everything about this place.'

I looked at the six cows in a row. 'Didn't you say that you couldn't afford to keep her?' I asked, worried.

'That's right, but I've had an idea,' the farmer replied. 'I can put two or three calves on to her instead of milking her. The old stable across the yard is empty and she can live in there quite happily.'

'What a wonderful idea, Mr Dakin. She'll be very comfortable there and she'd suckle three calves easily. She would probably pay her way.'

'Well, I'm not worried about that,' said the farmer smiling. 'After all these years, she doesn't owe me anything. The important thing is that Blossom has come home.'